WILLY HELPS A FRIEND

STACEY ANN BEITLER

Eloquent Books

Eloquent Books
An imprint of Strategic Book Group
P.O. Box 333
Durham CT 06422
www.StrategicBookGroup.com

ISBN: 978-1-60911-355-1

Printed in the United States of America

In loving memory of my father,

Willy Melikian,

who was a friend to all he met.

Willy the worm had been living on the MacDonald's farm for quite some time now and was beginning to get used to his new home. There were so many new friends to meet and learn about everyday. Each new friend had a new talent to share and was eager to learn more about Willy.

One day, while passing by the haystack, he heard the sound of someone crying.

"Why are you crying?" asked Willy.

Through tear filled eyes, Skunk sobbed, "I'm new here. It seems like no one wants to be my friend."

Willy was surprised to hear this; especially since the animals were so nice to him when he first came to the farm. "What makes you say that?" asked Willy curiously.

"Haven't you heard my part in the song?" asked Skunk.

Old MacDonald had a farm,
E-I-E-I-O!
And on his farm he had a skunk,
E-I-E-I-O!
With a spray spray here, and a spray spray there,
Here a spray. There a spray,
Everywhere a spray-spray.
Old MacDonald had a farm,
E-I-E-I-O!

"Whenever I try to make a friend, they run away from me," said Skunk. "It's not the first time this has happened to me. As soon as anyone realizes I'm a skunk, they don't even give me a chance."

"Well, my name is Willy and I'm not running away. I'll be your friend. I'm sure you will make lots of friends here," said Willy reassuringly.

"Really?" said Skunk, wiping her eyes.

"Really," said Willy.

Willy decided to get to the bottom of this himself. He would talk to the other animals. There had to be an explanation for their behavior.

"Have you seen Skunk?" asked Willy.

"Why are you looking for her?" asked Pig in surprise.

"Oh, no particular reason," replied Willy.

"If I was you, I wouldn't be looking for her," continued Pig. "She might spray you."

"Why would she spray me?" asked Willy.

"I don't know. But I'm not taking any chances!" exclaimed Pig.

7

"Do you know where I could find Skunk?" asked Willy.

"Why would I know where she is?" replied Swan in disgust. "I stay as far away from her as possible!"

"Why?" inquired Willy.

"I heard she'll spray you just for fun," said Swan.

"Really?" said Willy in disbelief.
"Who told you that?"

"Oh, everyone knows that!"
proclaimed Swan as she turned
and glided gracefully
away.

8

"Did Skunk pass by here?" asked Willy.

"Why? Are you expecting her to pass by here?" exclaimed Squirrel.

"Maybe," said Willy.

Squirrel began to nervously collect his nuts.

"Wait, where are you going?"

"Didn't you hear? If you even look at her, she'll spray you!"

"No!" cried Willy. "That is not true!"

"Oh it's true," continued Squirrel. "So I'm making sure that I am nowhere near her!" And he scurried away.

"Have you seen Skunk anywhere?" asked Willy.

"No," giggled the monkeys.

"What's so funny?" asked Willy.

"Don't you mean have we smelled Skunk anywhere?" chuckled the monkeys.

"What do you mean?" asked Willy.

"She smells **stinky!**" laughed the monkeys as they tumbled away.

Willy was shocked to learn that each animal he spoke with had the same opinion of Skunk, but none of the animals had ever even met her!

Willy had to do something! So he decided to call a farm meeting.

All of the animals assembled near the old stump wondering who had called the meeting. When it seemed as if all the animals had arrived, Willy began to speak.

"I called this meeting on behalf of Skunk," began Willy, as Skunk poked her head out from behind a nearby tree.

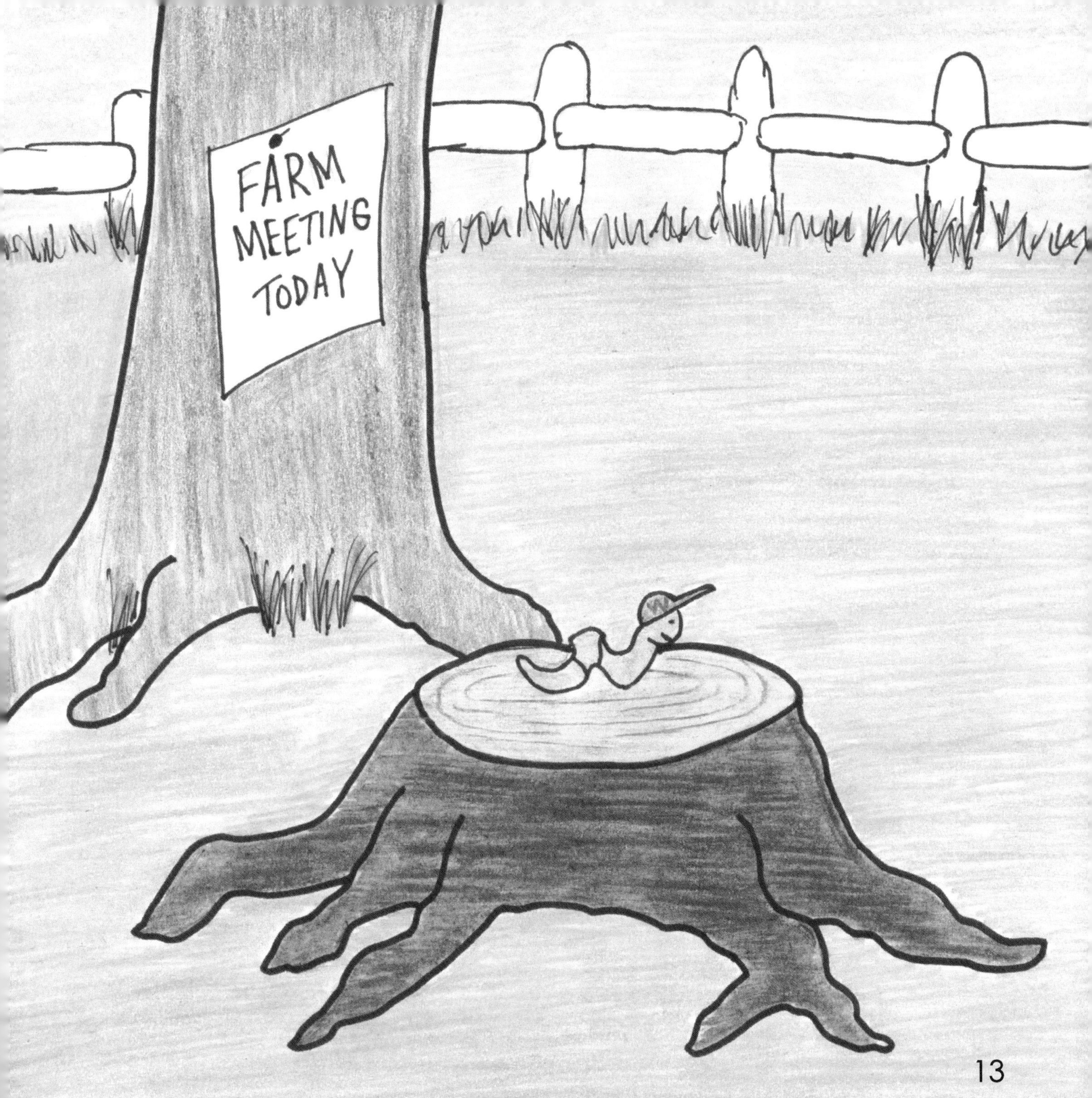
FARM
MEETING
TODAY

Some animals gasped.

Others lowered their eyes.

Squirrel even fainted!

Willy continued. He was determined to show the other animals the truth about Skunk. "I'd like to introduce you all to my friend, Skunk." Skunk joined Willy on the old stump. "Why don't' you tell everyone a little bit about yourself?" said Willy.

"Well," began Skunk shyly, "I like to sleep a lot during the day."

"Hmmm," thought Raccoon and Fox. "We like to sleep during the day too."

"One of my favorite foods is fruit," continued Skunk.

"Wow!" thought the monkeys. "We like fruit too!"

"I love making new friends, but I like to spend time alone too," added Skunk.

"I like my alone time too," thought Panda.

"I've always been
misunderstood,"
said Skunk sadly.
"You see there's this
thing I do, when I'm
scared. First I raise
my tail. Then I look
around to see if I'm
in danger. If I think
I am, then I spray a
really stinky spray."
"You don't do it just
for fun?" asked Pig.
"Or to be mean?"
asked Squirrel.
"Of course not!"
cried Skunk.

Maybe the animals had been wrong about Skunk.

Porcupine remembered what it felt like when the other animals were afraid of his quills. He would never poke anyone intentionally!

Bee thought of how upset he got when he was swatted at or run away from when he was just trying to say hello. He would only sting if it was absolutely necessary!

Pig remembered how some animals didn't want to get too close to him because he was dirty. He only rolled in the mud to stay cool!

Everyone thought the monkeys were all fun and games. They did have a serious side.

So many people were afraid of mouse . . . and she didn't even know why!
As Skunk continued, the other animals' expressions of fear and disgust were slowly replaced by curiosity and calm.

After getting to know Skunk, the animals realized that she wasn't much different than all of them.

"You mean you don't smell stinky all the time?" asked the monkeys.

"Not that I know of," shrugged Skunk.

The animals decided that, with the exception of surprise visits, surprise parties, or any kind of surprise for that matter, there was no reason at all to be afraid of their new friend Skunk.

Old MacDonald had a farm,
E-I-E-I-O!
And on that farm he had a skunk,
E-I-E-I-O!
When they take the time
The animals find
Skunk is not what they had in mind.
Old MacDonald had a farm,
E-I-E-I-O!

25

LaVergne, TN USA
15 February 2011
216459LV00002B